First U.S. edition 2002

Printed in Hong Kong

2 4 6 8 10 9 7 5 3 1

For each other – V. S. & J. S.

Library of Congress Cataloging-in-Publication Data
Schwarz, Viviane. The adventures of a nose / Viviane Schwarz ; Joel Stewart [illustrator].
—1st U.S. ed. p. cm. Summary: The Nose searches all over the world for a place where he can both fit in and stick out, a place where he can be happy.
ISBN 0-7636-1674-5 [1. Nose—Fiction. 2. Identity—Fiction.] I. Stewart, Joel, ill. II. Title. PZ7.S41145 Who 2002 [E]—dc21 2001025682

This book was typeset in Dickens.

Text copyright © 2002 by Silvia T. Viviane Schwarz

The illustrations were done in mixed media

Illustrations copyright © 2002 by Joel Stewart

Candlewick Press 2067 Massachusetts Avenue

Cambridge, Massachusetts 02140

visit us at www.candlewick.com

The Adventures of a Nose

Viviane Schwarz

illustrated by Joel Stewart

CANDLEWICK PRESS
CAMBRIDGE, MASSACHUSETTS

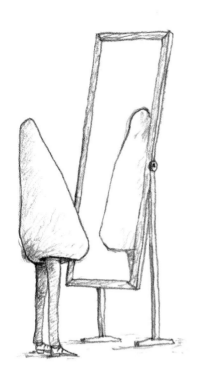

Thisisthe
Nose, thinking,
"Somewhere in the
world must be a place just for me.
A place where I can fit in, and stick out.
I could be really happy there!"

He goes to the city.
Everything is big
and smells exciting.
The Nose sniffs
up and down the
streets until he is
completely lost.
"You look confused,"
calls a cat from
the city library.
"Come in here!
Here you can find things out,"
says the library cat.

The Nose likes books.
"This one smells of ink, and
this one smells of dust," he thinks.
"Hmm. Maybe
I could stay here."
But he can't.
The library closes at night, and
everyone has to leave.
Where now?
"I know the best place
in the world," says a dog.
"Come with me!"

They go to a restaurant.
"Smells wonderful," says the Nose.
"But what am I supposed to do here?"
The dog doesn't reply
because he is too busy eating.
"This is a place for mouths,"
thinks the Nose, "not for me."
"I think you are fabulous!" says a pigeon.
"You should be famous—come with me!"
Maybe the pigeon knows
the right place for a Nose?

This is the Pigeon Theater.
The Nose is doing a beautiful sneezing dance.
The pigeons cry, "Bravo!"
"They are all looking at me," worries the Nose.
"It makes me feel like there is something
nasty sticking to me."
So he sneaks out and runs away,
out of the city.

This is the Nose feeling much better.
"The world is big," he thinks.
"There must be a place for me
somewhere. I will find it for myself."

The Nose climbs up,
high as the mountains
and the birds and the clouds.

He dives down,
deep as the fish
and the lowest
valleys of the sea.

Should he stay
where it's clear,
cold, and tingly?

Should he stay
where it's spicy and hot?

This is the Nose feeling much worse.
He has traveled all around the world.
He has smelled amazing things.
"But I still haven't found my place,"
he thinks. "A place to fit in and stick out.
A place to be really happy.
Maybe there's something
wrong with me."

The Nose

goes to see a doctor.

"I just don't fit in anywhere,"
the Nose sniffles.

"Oh, I think you do!" the doctor says.

"Don't you see? The whole world fits

perfectly around YOU.

Your place is always in

the middle sticking out —

because you are a Nose!"

This is the Nose who has
smelled the whole world
and has found his place in it—
he fits in by sticking out, always.

"Of course!" he thinks.
"How wonderful!"